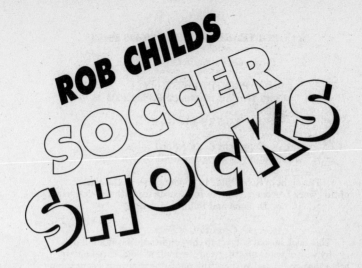

ROB CHILDS
SOCCER SHOCKS

ILLUSTRATED BY
JON RILEY

CORGI YEARLING BOOKS

A CORGI YEARLING BOOK : 0 440 864038

First publication in Great Britain

PRINTING HISTORY
Corgi Yearling edition published 2001

1 3 5 7 9 10 8 6 4 2

Copyright © 2001 Rob Childs
Illustrations copyright © 2001 by Jon Riley

Set in 12/15pt New Century Schoolbook
by Phoenix Typesetting, Ilkley, West Yorkshire

Corgi Books are published by Transworld Publishers,
61–63 Uxbridge Road, London W5 5SA,
a division of The Random House Group Ltd,
in Australia by Random House Australia (Pty) Ltd,
20 Alfred Street, Milsons Point, Sydney, NSW 2061, Australia,
in New Zealand by Random House New Zealand Ltd,
18 Poland Road, Glenfield, Auckland 10, New Zealand
and in South Africa by Random House (Pty) Ltd,
Endulini, 5a Jubilee Road, Parktown 2193, South Africa

Made and printed in Great Britain by
Cox & Wyman plc, Reading, Berkshire.

Especially for all soccer teachers and coaches

1 Sweeper System

'Watch it! Here comes Tubs,' warned Sanjay from his goal. 'Better hide any choc you've got left.'

'Wonder how many eggs Tubs scoffed this Easter?' laughed Titch as the roly-poly defender waddled across the village recreation ground towards the group of footballers.

The goalkeeper grinned. 'Tons, I bet. He's even shaped like one.'

Luke Crawford glanced at the time. 'C'mon, Tubs, you should've been here a quarter of an hour ago,' he called out, trying to exert his non-existent authority as captain. 'What's kept you?'

Tubs didn't respond till he reached the pitch

and leant on the goalpost, which creaked and shifted under his weight. 'Dinner,' he grunted.

'Careful, Tubs!' cried Sanjay, supporting the woodwork. 'I need my goal in one piece for Sunday's game.'

'Huh! Pity you don't protect it better during matches,' he snorted, giving the post a sly kick before moving away.

'You can be on my side,' Luke decided. 'We're a man short.'

'Yeah, I've seen Titch,' Tubs smirked. 'But where's the rest of 'em?'

'Thought Ricki was supposed to be here today as well,' Sanjay put in, gazing into the distance where the Garner twins were battling for possession of the ball. The other players had taken the chance to slump onto the ground, content to wait until either Gary or Gregg returned in triumph.

'So did I,' Luke admitted. 'I rang Ricki up a couple of days ago to remind him about the practice. Said I'd got big plans for him.'

Tubs let out his rumbling laugh. 'Well, that explains it, then. Your cousin's got more sense than I gave him credit. He knows when it's best to stay away.'

Privately, Luke was quite encouraged that so many of his squad had bothered to turn up for training in the school holidays. He liked to think it showed their commitment to playing for Swillsby Swifts, the under-13 Sunday League team of soccer misfits that he'd formed at the start of the season. Running his own team was the only way that Luke could guarantee himself a regular game of football.

'Er . . . what exactly are these big plans of yours, anyway?' asked Sanjay warily. 'Isn't it a bit late to start devising new tactics?'

'Never too late for making improvements,' Luke beamed. 'We've got to make sure we pick

up the extra points we need to steer clear of relegation.'

'And how many more do we need, d'yer reckon?'

Luke was usually vague – or evasive – on this touchy subject, making sure the other players never saw the updated league table that he received in the post every week. He gave a little shrug. 'Not many.'

'How many?' Tubs insisted.

'Look out!' Sanjay yelled. 'Here he comes.'

'Who?' demanded Titch. 'Friend or foe?'

'How should I know?' replied the goalkeeper as one of the twins ran towards them. 'Just go and stop him.'

'He might be on my side.'

'He *is* on your side,' Luke told him. 'It's Gary.'

Titch was impressed. 'How d'yer know that?'

'Gary's got a left foot. Look at the way he dribbles with it. Gregg only uses *his* left to fill the other boot.'

'Well, don't just give him a free shot at goal, whoever he is,' Sanjay kept on. 'Somebody go and get in his way.'

Tubs took the instruction literally. He'd found from experience that the best method of dealing with fast, tricky opponents was simply to stand in their way. So that's what he did. He positioned

himself right in Gary's flightpath and nobody blocked the route to goal better than Tubs. Head down, the onrushing Gary cannoned into Tubs at full throttle and bounced away as if from the cushion of a snooker table.

The ball ran loose to Luke and the skipper broke into his habitual commentary mode to describe – or at least interpret – the ensuing action.

'. . . *And now the Swifts player-manager, Luke Crawford, moves smoothly on to the ball . . .*' (he trod on it and stumbled)

'. . . *and finds himself on his own with no support . . .*' (everyone else was watching – and listening – with amusement)

'*. . . the skipper dummies one way and then the other to wrong-foot the defence . . .*' (he and the ball went in different directions)

'*. . . and then cuts inside onto his trusty right foot . . .*' (both of his feet were about as trustworthy as leaving Tubs in charge of the school tuck shop)

'*. . . the striker looks up to see the goalie straying off his line and then coolly picks his spot . . .*' (Sanjay had moved to one side to give Luke the whole goal to aim at)

'*. . . chipping the ball over the keeper's head towards the top corner of the net . . .*' (he sliced it up into the air towards the far corner of the recky)

'*. . . and the crowd goes wild with delight . . .*' (the other players rolled about in uncontrolled hilarity as Luke charged after the stray ball, still broadcasting his own version of events to the world).

Ricki arrived half an hour later. He hadn't missed all that much action. His teammates were sprawled on the grass again, taking yet another breather.

13

'Sorry about time,' Ricki began, spreading his hands in a gesture of helplessness. 'My father is plenty mad – the car break down, y'know . . .'

'Don't worry about it, Ricki,' said Tubs. 'Crawford things never work properly.'

'My name is Fortuna,' Ricki corrected him. 'My father, he is Italian.'

'Yeah, we know that, but your mother's got no excuse. She comes with the family jinx.'

'*Jinx?* What is this jinx?'

'It's another word we have round here for Crawford.'

Luke gave Tubs a dirty look. 'Don't listen to him, Ricki,' he said. 'We're just glad to have you here.'

'Got bad news,' he said, squatting next to his cousin. 'My father says we must be going home soon.'

'But you've only just got here,' Luke protested. 'I want us to work on some new tactics before we pack up.'

'No, I mean really go home,' Ricki explained. 'To Roma.'

'What!' cried Luke, jumping to his feet in alarm. 'You *can't* do that. It's not the end of the season yet. We need you.'

'I am plenty sorry, Luke – I want to stay, y'know, but . . .'

Sanjay interrupted. 'You mean you'd rather play for the Swifts than go back to sunny Italy?' he said in disbelief. 'You must be as daft as the rest of the family after all!'

Luke decided the best way to relieve his frustrations, as always, was to kick a ball about. It didn't seem to matter too much that the ball rarely went where he intended, just so long as it *went* – and so that he could go and miskick it again somewhere else.

'C'mon, you lot, on your feet,' he called out. 'We've got work to do.'

There were grumbles all round.

'Aw, Skipper, I was just gettin' comfy,' complained Dazza, whom Luke had been trying unsuccessfully to convert from winger to wing-back.

'Yeah, we've done enough running about for one day,' said Tubs.

Luke tried to haul Tubs to his feet, but quickly realized that was a waste of effort. He'd need a crane to help him. 'You haven't done any running about yet, Tubs,' he pointed out. 'You never do.'

Tubs' full-moon face creased up. 'That's my motto,' he chuckled. 'Don't run before you can walk.'

Eventually, under protest, the players stirred

themselves and let Luke explain his latest plans. The Swifts had changed their tactical formations this season more times than Tubs broke into a sweat during a game.

'We're going to use a sweeper system in our next match, I've got it all worked out,' Luke gabbled. 'And Ricki here is going to be our sweeper.'

Ricki looked as puzzled as the rest. 'Me, sweeper?' he queried. 'You mean I need a brush?'

'Only to clear up the plenty big mess we're in,' Tubs grunted.

Luke ignored the jibe. 'No, it means I want you to play deeper than usual, behind the main markers, dealing with anything that gets past them.'

'Who are our main markers?' put in Sanjay. 'I didn't know we had any.'

'Ha! Ha! Very funny,' retorted Big Ben, their centre-back, pretending to look hurt. 'It's about time we had a bit of extra help in defence.'

'You'll soon see how it works, Ricki,' Luke assured him. 'Just stay back and cover the others, OK? Put yourself about plenty.'

'Ah, got it. I put myself about plenty good. I like the sound of that.'

Ricki scampered around like a playful puppy in the short session that followed, eager to

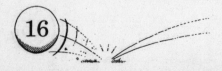

please, but he rarely popped up in the places Luke wanted him to be – that is, wherever the ball was.

'I try my best, Luke, yes?' Ricki said. 'It's just that rugby is my game, you know that. I not really understand soccer rules.'

'Join the club, Ricki, old mate,' chortled Tubs. 'Neither do we.'

The practice fizzled out after the Garner twins had to go home early and Titch also made an excuse to leave.

'Got to take my goldfish out for a walk,' he said before trailing away.

'Big game on Sunday,' Luke reminded the others. 'Vital league points at stake.'

'Who we playing?' asked Brain.

'Don't you ever read the fixture book?' Luke replied, then realized who had spoken. Brian Draper, the Swifts' one truly talented player, didn't read anything unless he had to, due to his dyslexic difficulties. 'Sorry, Brain, it's a home match here against Southcote United. Two o'clock kick-off.'

'How many did we lose by at their place?' asked Dazza.

'Who said we lost?'

'Just take it for granted. So what was the score, then?'

Luke mumbled something that no-one heard.

'Er, sorry, Skipper,' smirked Big Ben. 'Didn't quite catch that.'

'Um . . . I'll have to check,' Luke said, pretending to be untying his laces.

'Rubbish!' exclaimed Tubs. 'You know all the results off by heart. You've got 'em logged in that little black book of yours.'

How the other players would love to get hold of that record book! They knew Luke used it to keep not only the statistical details of every match, but also to write up fanciful reports of his own contributions to the action.

'Double figures, I bet,' grinned Dazza. 'The only time the skipper ever goes quiet is when he's asked about the scores.'

'It wasn't double figures, if you must know,' Luke sneered. 'It was only seven.'

'Oh, well, that's all right, then. They must have hit us on a good day.'

'Well, they won't even know what's hit *them* this time,' Luke said with determination. 'We've improved loads since that first meeting.'

Tubs let out a loud guffaw. 'Save the fiction for your little black book, Skipper. We're gonna get thrashed again, admit it. We don't mind.'

'No, we won't,' said Luke, standing up, his face flushed. 'Not with our new sweeper system in operation. They won't be able to work that out.'

'Well, that'll make things fair, then,' Tubs grinned. ''Cos nor can we!'

2 Distractions

The match against Southcote United may well have kicked off in the afternoon, but the Swifts still managed to look half asleep.

United shook the home side roughly out of their slumbers with a goal in the very first minute and soon grabbed another from a corner. The only times Sanjay had been able to get his hands on the ball was when he bent to pick it out of the net.

'Wake up!' cried Luke's father. 'You're letting them walk all over us.'

'No change there, then,' murmured Uncle Ray, taking off his glasses to wipe them. 'Teams have been using us as a doormat all season.'

'I shouldn't put your specs back on, if I were you,' said his brother. 'Things may not look quite so bad without them.'

'I won't be able to see a thing.'

'Exactly! Lucky you.'

The Crawford brothers were officially in charge of the Swifts, having their names in the league handbook as manager and secretary, but that was only for form's sake – or for the work of filling in forms. They left all the coaching to the skipper. In theory, at least, Luke was in full control. In practice, and even more so in games, things were invariably out of control.

'C'mon, defence, sort out the marking,' the player-manager complained. 'Who's supposed to be picking up that big number eight at corners?'

The defenders looked round at each other, hoping somebody else might be willing to take the blame. Nobody was. They were all far better at passing the buck than passing the ball.

'Thought the sweeper was gonna take care of anybody who's free,' grumbled Tubs. 'He's our spare man.'

'There were two Reds,' Ricki protested. 'I cannot mark both.'

'Shame how you chose the wrong one,' Tubs retorted.

Any intended irony was wasted on Ricki. It went right over his head, much like the ball had done.

Despite the poor start, Luke was prepared to be more tolerant. He wanted to give his new system every chance to be a success before it was thrown onto the Swifts' ever-growing tactical scrapheap.

Luke gave Ricki a slap on the back in encouragement. 'Not your fault,' he said. 'Bound to be a few teething troubles at first.'

'Teething troubles?' Ricki repeated.

'Um . . . yeah, y'know, like a baby has,' Luke replied hesitantly, sensing that Ricki would still have no idea what he was trying to say. 'Um . . . you can't expect things to work out right straightaway. Needs time . . .'

Time was just one crucial factor the Swifts did not have in their favour, either in this match or in what little was left of the season. Another was skill – a vital commodity also in very short supply in the Swifts' changing room, and even more obviously missing out on the pitch.

After such a flying start, United may have been guilty of coasting and only scored once more before the interval. And with their minds perhaps on the half-time refreshments, they even allowed the Swifts to pull a goal back. The visitors defended a corner sloppily, letting the ball skid right through the penalty area to an opponent lurking near the right touchline.

The main reason Tubs was there was to be the nearest to the trays of orange segments when the whistle blew. Annoyed by the distraction from the food, he lashed the ball back across the area where it was met by a spectacular diving header.

Ricki had arrived late, unnoticed, to join the attack and threw himself forward at the leather missile. Only at the last split second did he head it rather than make a rugby-style catch. The ball thudded against the far post and Dazza gleefully lashed the rebound high into the roof of the net.

'GOAL!!' screamed the player-commentator. *'What a time to score! It's only 3–1 now and there's no doubt who will enjoy the oranges more during the break – they're bound to taste all the sweeter to the Swifts . . .'*

Tubs could already tell everyone how sweet they were. He celebrated the goal by helping himself from one of the trays.

'OK, men, listen,' said Luke. 'I reckon it's just a matter of time before we score another goal. We've got them rattled, I can tell . . .'

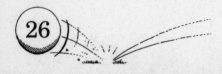

Luke trailed off, realizing he was talking to himself. His teammates' attention was fixed elsewhere and even the few remaining scraps of orange lay neglected on the ground.

'Who's that?'

'Dunno – never seen her before.'

'Must be with one of the Southcote mob.'

'Doubt it. She's heading straight for us.'

To the boys' astonishment, the girl in question was walking across the pitch and they instinctively huddled closer together for protection.

'What's she want with us?'

'Perhaps she's after our autographs?'

'She doesn't look that stupid.'

Ricki gave a little nervous cough. 'Um . . . sorry, you guys,' he faltered, beginning to redden. 'She is sort of with me, y'know.'

They stared at him with a mixture of new respect and suspicion.

'She from Italy, as well, then?' asked Gary.

'Um . . . no, she is in my class at school in Padley,' Ricki explained. 'She is giving me extra help with my English, see?'

Tubs nodded, his chins wobbling in agreement.

'I see, all right,' he said, giving Ricki a leer. 'She must be plenty good, yes?'

The boys were still laughing as the girl reached the group. 'Hi!' she greeted them confidently. Is the game over?'

'It is for us just about,' muttered Big Ben.

'No, it's not,' Luke stated defiantly. 'We're right back in it now and . . .'

The skipper was interrupted as usual, but this was the first time that his attempted team talk had been stalled by a girl.

'You must be Luke,' she said, failing to hide a smirk.

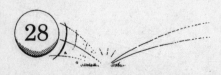

'Amazing!' gasped Sanjay. 'Your fame's spreading, Skipper. You're even getting recognized now.'

'Ricki's told me all about you,' she smiled, making Luke blush too.

'Soz, the skipper doesn't sign autographs till after the match,' said Gary, sidling up to her. 'Er, didn't catch your name . . .'

'It's Laura. Mind if I borrow Ricki for a minute?'

'So long as you let us have him back for the second half. He's our sweeper.'

'Sweeper?'

'Yeah, don't worry about it,' Gary grinned. 'None of us really understands what it means, either.'

Laura led an embarrassed Ricki a little distance away but, try as they might, his teammates could not overhear what was being said.

'What's she after?' grunted Mark, the centre-back. 'Hasn't Ricki done his homework or something?'

'She can keep me behind after school any time,' Gary grinned, nudging his twin. 'How about you, Junior?'

Gregg pulled a face. He didn't like it when Gary used that pet nickname to emphasize the ten minutes' seniority that Gary claimed over him.

'I wouldn't know,' Gregg replied sourly. 'I haven't got your experience.'

The referee's whistle cut short any further speculation and half-time ended without Luke having been able to make any of the coaching points he'd considered vital. But that was normal, anyway. The players always seemed to find something else of greater interest to distract them.

'C'mon, Ricki!' Luke called out in frustration.

'Time's up, number four, come on in,' chortled Tubs. 'Business before pleasure.'

As Laura went to stand on the touchline, the Swifts refused to budge until Ricki rejoined them.

'Well?' demanded Mark.

'Well what?' said Ricki.

'What did she want?'

The referee gave another impatient beep.

'C'mon, men!' Luke urged. 'We've got work to do. We can still win this game.'

'Belt up, Skipper, this is important,' said Tubs. 'C'mon, Ricki – spill the beans.'

Ricki looked blank. 'Spill the beans?'

'Oh, ignore Tubs, he's always going on about food,' grinned Gary. 'Just tell us what your friend Laura had to say.'

'She has invited me to her home for tea,' he explained. 'Her parents, they want to meet me.'

'Bet Tubs wishes he could meet a girl like that, inviting him for tea on their first date,' joked Sanjay.

''Fraid you've had it now, mate,' said Gary, draping an arm around Ricki in mock consolation.

'Why is that?'

'It's an old English custom of ours,' he replied,

31

trying hard to keep a straight face. 'Getting invited to meet the folks is just the first step.'

'First step?'

'Yeah – towards getting married!' Gary exclaimed. 'Congratulations!'

3 Party-Poopers

The Swifts played the second half with the equivalent of ten and a half men – nine and a half if you discounted the skipper, which was usually wise.

Ricki was mentally absent and Luke, well, Luke was just mental. The other players were made aware of Luke's physical presence by an irritating droning noise in their ears – his running commentary on the game that was swirling around him.

'With their sweeper having gone walkabout upfield, the skipper now has to fill in for the wandering star, sacrificing himself for the good of the team. Fortuna's way out of position as a

Swifts attack breaks down and the red shirts of United surge forward once more. The winger races past Gary Garner and cuts into the box, but the skipper glides across to intercept and plug the gap. He times his tackle to perfection . . . aaahhh!'

'Penalty!' went up the United chorus as the winger sprawled full-length over Luke's outstretched leg.

'Huh! Nice one, Skipper!' groaned Sanjay, as the referee pointed to the penalty spot. 'That's a real big help.'

The goalkeeper had been in this one-against-one situation many times during the course of the season. With a heavy sigh of resignation, he positioned himself on his line, mercifully out of reception range of Luke's on-going description of the scene from the edge of the penalty area.

'. . . and the kicker runs confidently in, doing a little jink in his curved approach to try and fool the keeper. He blasts the ball and – oh! It struck the post and rebounded into the keeper's arms. Sanjay Mistry never even made a move for the ball. Just the kind of break the plucky Swifts deserve . . .'

Sanjay hoofed the ball away upfield, but his relief was only temporary. The ball was lobbed straight back into the goalmouth to the very boy who had just missed the penalty and he took

immediate revenge by smacking it past the help-less Sanjay.

Peeeeeppppp!!

'*No goal!*' cried the commentator. '*The ref's disallowed it for offside. Thanks to the skipper's quick thinking, he's saved his team from falling further behind. The emergency sweeper urged his defence to move out after the penalty drama and the striker was caught in their well-practised offside trap . . .*'

The reality, as always, was somewhat different. The Swifts defenders wouldn't recognize an offside trap if it sprang up and bit them on the nose. Fortune, if not Fortuna, was

smiling on them for once. The Reds striker had been too busy sulking after his miss and had mooched away from goal even slower than Tubs. He was now doubly guilty of letting the Swifts off the hook.

Five minutes later, the Swifts made him feel even worse. The Garner twins linked up almost telepathically in midfield, playing a neat one-two exchange that sent Gregg galloping goalwards. He rather went and spoiled things by tripping over outside the penalty area, but the ball ran free to Brain who cut in from the left wing to shoot home with a right-foot drive.

'3–2! The Swifts fightback has sure got the United players worried. You can see it in their body language. They know they've got a real match on their hands now. Their faces look strained, their shoulders have slumped, their legs are feeling like lead and their hearts must be pounding . . .'

Given the opportunity, the commentator might well have worked his way through most of the opposition's body parts – including the rude bits – but his attention was caught by a commotion on the touchline. Ricki seemed to have got himself involved in a brawl.

'You want to get yourself sent off?' cried Big Ben, who was helping to drag Ricki away. 'What d'yer think you're doing?'

'These two,' Ricki protested, jabbing an accusing finger at the United substitutes. 'They pester Laura.'

'I could have dealt with them myself, thanks,' she said hotly. 'You've only gone and made things worse.'

Big Ben guided the crestfallen Ricki back onto the pitch. 'C'mon, this is no time to play the gallant Latin lover,' he said. 'You're supposed to be playing football.'

'See you after the match, yes?' Ricki called to her.

Laura shook her head. 'No, I have to get back home now. Dad's waiting in the car. See you at the party later, OK?'

'Party?' repeated Big Ben. 'Thought you said it was just for tea.'

Ricki shrugged. 'She not want to invite all of you as well.'

'Charming! She didn't want any riff-raff, is that it?'

'Riff-raff?'

'Yeah, like us Swifts,' explained Tubs. 'Can't say I blame her really.'

'We're not riff-raff,' Luke objected. 'If anybody treats us like that, they're in for a shock. Look at United. They're all getting at each other now, panicking 'cos they know we can beat 'em.'

'More like Dis-United!' joked Titch.

'Right, let's go for that equalizer, team,' cried Luke, rallying his forces. 'And then the winner!'

To give the Swifts due credit, they did try their best and went close to scoring an all-important third goal, one that might well have led to them snatching all three precious points. A shot from Gregg skimmed just wide of a post and the goalie was fortunate in blocking Brain's volley with his legs. Sadly, however, that was about as good as it got.

The visitors managed to rally their forces and

put the match effectively beyond reach with an
excellent fourth goal. Only two fine saves from
Sanjay near the end prevented United from adding further to their tally, but the Swifts were far
from downhearted. The players knew they'd
given a good account of themselves, despite the
final result.

'Never mind, Skip, we nearly did it,' said Dazza
as they trooped off the pitch. 'At least you'll be
able to give us a good write-up now in that little
black book of yours.'

Dazza giggled and headed for the changing
cabin, leaving the player-manager to ponder
over what might have been.

'Nearly's not good enough,' he sighed. 'You don't get any points for *nearly*. That's why we're down at the bottom of the table.'

Before tea, Luke went to his room to bring his personal record book up to date. Personal, because the exaggerated accounts of his performances were meant for *his* eyes only, and also because hardly anybody else normally managed to get a mention. He could make any defeat, no matter how catastrophic, sound almost like a

victory. United were very lucky, in this book, even to end up winning.

Luke had to be a little more circumspect, if not exactly accurate, in his next piece of sports reporting. This was more for public consumption, if anybody else apart from his teammates ever bothered to read it.

Uncle Ray was the editor of the village's free newspaper, the *Swillsby Chronicle*, and allowed Luke space for match reports – often testing Ray's editorial skills to the limit in deciding how much of Luke's biased and semi-fictional prose could actually be printed.

It was a task that Luke loved, even if he did regret that he could rarely report on a Swifts triumph. He scribbled a few thoughts down on a piece of notepaper then settled himself at the keyboard of his computer.

So Near, Yet So Far

by our soccer correspondent

Swillsby Swifts 2 – 4 Southcote United

The Swifts player-manager Luke Crawford described this setback as the win-that-got-away. His team showed great spirit after falling

behind to early goals and deserved at least a point to help their crusade against relegation.

'Our new sweeper system still needs a little bit more fine-tuning to work smoothly,' the coach admitted, 'but the lads are confident they can put things right before their next key fixture.'

Strikes from David 'Dazza' Richards and Brian 'Brain' Draper brought the battling Swifts right back into this match, but a crowd disturbance proved something of a distraction and United managed to hang on to their slim lead.

'Don't write us off yet,' said the skipper. 'The party isn't over till the man in black blows the final whistle! We will survive!'

4 Summer Term

'Wonder what all that noise is?' said Gary as he and Sean strolled past the P.E. shed at lunchtime on the first day of term.

'Dunno, and I don't care,' replied Sean, throwing his crisps packet down onto the playground.

'What's the matter with you? You sound as grumpy as old Frosty.'

'School! That's what's the matter with me. Having to come back to this dump when I could still be lying in bed like in the holidays.'

'Frosty' Winter, head of Swillsby Comprehensive's P.E. Department, suddenly emerged from the shed, brushing off the remains of a cobweb

from his hair. Gary gulped, hoping the teacher hadn't overheard his remark.

'You two!' Frosty barked. 'Come here.'

'It wasn't me, sir,' Gary said guiltily.

'What wasn't you?'

'Um . . . whatever you think I might have done, sir.'

Frosty sighed. 'That's your new policy, is it . . . er . . . ?' he began before stalling. He still couldn't tell the difference between the Garner twins, even at close quarters.

'He's Gregg, sir,' Sean put in helpfully, just in case Gary was going to get blamed for something.

'I knew that, thank you,' Frosty replied tetchily. 'It's your new policy, is it, Gregg, to deny something even before you've been accused? You're as bad as your brother.'

Gary wasn't sure whether or not to take that as a compliment. 'Oh, I'm not as bad as all that, sir,' he said innocently.

Frosty couldn't be bothered to pursue the matter. 'Come in here, both of you,' he ordered. 'I've got a job for you.'

The boys groaned inwardly. By the state of Frosty's tracksuit, it looked like it might well be a very dirty job. Sean was especially displeased. He prided himself on his immaculate appearance.

'Oh, and Sean . . .' Frosty added over his shoulder as he led the way in.

'Yes, sir,' replied Sean eagerly, hoping he might be given something else – less messy – to do instead.

'. . . Pick up that crisps packet first that you just dropped.'

The teacher had been struggling to sort out the sports equipment that would be needed in the new term. Sets of cricket stumps, bats and pads, many with buckles missing, were strewn over the shed floor along with javelins, discuses, shot puts, tape measures and relay batons.

Sean eyed the dirty pads with distaste. 'Don't fancy wearing any of them,' he muttered. 'Looks like something's been chewing them.'

'They were already like that last year,' said Gary.

'Aye, and they'll be like that next year too,' rasped Frosty. 'School can't afford to buy new ones. C'mon, give me a hand with these things.'

Frosty began to haul at sets of hurdles, cursing under his breath as they kept getting trapped by each other and by other pieces of apparatus.

'Some fool just chucked 'em in here at the end of last summer and didn't bother to stack them properly,' he muttered by way of explanation. 'Thank God it's the last time I'll have to do this chore.'

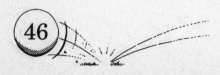

The boys glanced at each other. 'Er . . . why's that, sir?' asked Gary.

Frosty forced two hurdles apart. 'Oh, nothing,' he replied, trying to pass it off. 'Put this lot outside and make more room for all the cricket stuff.'

'What d'yer reckon?' hissed Gary as they propped the hurdles on the grass.

'I reckon it's about time old Frosty learnt to say *please*,' Sean grumbled, picking a piece of dirt off his trousers. 'These things are filthy.'

'Never mind them. I mean, about what he just said – about this being the last time?'

Sean gave a little shrug. 'Who knows? Maybe he's gonna store them somewhere else.'

'Don't be a moron. That was just an excuse.'

'So what? Let's just shift the hurdles and perhaps he'll let us go then.'

'Got a feeling it might just be Frosty who's going.'

'How d'yer mean?'

'Well, y'know – leaving or something.'

Sean pulled a face. 'More like retiring, if you ask me. He must be at least a hundred!'

Their speculation was cut short. 'Oi! C'mon, you two – get a move on,' thundered a voice from deep inside the shed. 'I don't want to be here for ever.'

47

It was a time in schools when the seasons over-lapped for a short while. Goalposts stayed up long enough to play any outstanding soccer matches, but there were also the conflicting interests of summer sports like cricket and athletics that demanded space on the playing fields.

Frosty wanted the football finished and out of the way as soon as possible. The under-13s had somehow managed to reach the Final of the local cup competition, despite the fact that over half the team was now made up of Swifts. Many other – better – players had been driven away by Frosty's bad temper and sarcasm.

Frostbite, as it was known, had recently claimed the Year 8 captain, Matthew Clarke, as its most notable victim, but it seemed to have little effect on the Swifts players who had grown more thick-skinned over the course of the season. Whatever they lacked in ability, they perhaps made up for to some extent in their enthusiasm for the game.

The skipper's armband had passed to Jon Crawford, Luke's talented cousin, who showed that he at least was on good form in a hastily arranged practice match against the Comp's Year 7 squad.

'*Johan's on the ball now,*' warbled Luke into his pretend microphone, a water bottle, as Jon broke free along the right wing. '*The defender's given him too much room, something I'm sure he's going to regret . . .*'

Even if the younger boy had been able to pick up Luke's touchline ramblings, he probably wouldn't have been aware that the pet nickname referred to a soccer legend who graced the game before any of them were born – Luke's hero, the great Dutch star of the 1970s, Johan Cruyff.

'*. . . Johan takes the full-back on at pace and sweeps past him as if he didn't exist. I doubt if the poor kid even knows where he's gone . . .*'

The new captain shaped to shoot as he reached the edge of the area, wrong-footing the keeper, but then slid the ball square to Brain instead to give his teammate the honour of drilling it low into the net.

'Good goal, lads,' Frosty called out, letting slip a piece of rare praise in recognition of the fact that the two players were his side's potential match-winners in the Final. In reality, they were the Comp's only hope of avoiding a heavy defeat against Grimthorpe School, who had already beaten them twice in the league.

The goal equalized the Year 7 team's opener when a long-distance shot had bobbled over Sanjay's ill-timed dive, and it soon paved the way for two more to give the older lads a deserved 3–1 advantage at half-time.

'Change ends quick,' Frosty bellowed. 'I want to get home soon.'

'Are we going to use any subs, sir?' asked Jon.

The teacher didn't need to follow his captain's gaze towards the touchline. He knew exactly to whom Jon was referring. 'Oh, I don't think we need to take such drastic measures yet, do you?' he said.

'It's only a practice, sir. You know how keen he is to get on the pitch.'

'Aye, I still have nightmares about it,' the

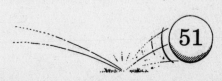

teacher grunted, attempting a piece of gruff humour. 'Oh, go on, then. If you want to – what do I care now?'

Jon gave his cousin a wave and Luke was pulling off his tracksuit top in an instant. Unfortunately, he'd forgotten that he still had the bottle in his hand and it got stuck halfway up his sleeve. The restart had to be delayed while the twins helped Luke to escape without breaking his arm.

'Who's going off, sir?' Luke asked as he ran on, his thin face flushed with excitement.

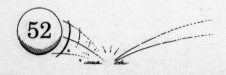

'Nobody.'

'But that means we'll have twelve men, sir. Won't that be an unfair advantage?'

'Only in theory,' came back the retort.

The Year 7 players might have complained if it had been anybody else but Luke Crawford. His fame – or infamy – spread well beyond the confines of his own year group in the school.

Not being allotted any particular position, Luke took that as a licence to roam, something that he always did anyway.

The experienced substitute has been given a floating role, to help out where most needed, and he's soon in the thick of the action, tracking back into his own penalty area . . .

'Get out of there!' barked Frosty, cutting off Luke's mobile commentary in mid-sentence. 'I don't want to see you anywhere near your own goal – got it? Stay upfield and make a nuisance of yourself in their half instead.'

That was something at least that Luke was very good at, making a nuisance of himself on the football field – and not only because of his knack of getting in other people's way . . .

'. . . *Luke Crawford drifts back upfield, unnoticed, like a phantom in the night, ghosting into space . . .*' whined his commentary, '. . . *they*

seek him here, they seek him there, they seek the unseen striker everywhere . . .'

Unseen, perhaps, but certainly not unheard. By the end of the game, the breathless voice-over had driven almost everybody to distraction. The only compensation for Luke's teammates was that they won – partly thanks to hardly allowing the substitute a kick – and for the younger losers in giving the source of their irritation as many kicks as possible.

5 Unlucky Luke

'What do you mean, this will be your last game?'

Ricki gave a shrug. 'I am plenty sorry, Luke,' he replied. 'My father, he say we have to go back to Roma next week.'

'But he promised me you'd be here till the end of the season.'

'Plans change,' Ricki said as an excuse. 'It is to do with business, y'know . . .'

Luke opened his mouth to speak again, but no sound came out. He was beside himself with frustration. He took a wild swing instead at a nearby ball and toppled over clumsily onto his backside.

'Uuurrgghhhh!'

He'd put his right hand into something soft and sticky – and he didn't need three guesses that it would be extremely smelly too.

'That's disgusting!' he complained, holding out his hand as if it didn't belong to him. 'Why don't some people clean up after their dogs?'

'What's the matter, Skipper?' asked Sean. 'Taking a break already?'

Luke pulled a face. 'Just give me a hand up, will you?'

'Sure . . .'

Luke saw the instant look of horror as Sean snatched his hand away a split second after making contact. He'd never heard such a fluent

stream of abuse leave Sean's lips and immediately regretted his action.

'I'm sorry, Sean, really I am,' he tried to apologize as his teammate turned to run back to the changing cabin. 'I just didn't think . . .'

It was too late for apologies. Luke sighed and got to his feet, unaided. 'Have to go and get cleaned up, too, I guess,' he said, glancing at his cousin.

'He was plenty mad,' Ricki said. 'Better find him, I think, before he goes home.'

Luke couldn't afford to lose anybody else. He charged back to the cabin at full speed.

'Wow! Just look at that boy go,' chortled Tubs from the pitch.

Big Ben laughed. 'He must have got caught short!'

'He ought to go in for the one hundred metres on Sports Day.'

'What event you going to do, Tubs?'

'Shot put, if old Frosty will let me. You only have to shuffle a few steps across the circle and then bung the thing as far as you can.'

'There must be a bit more to it than that.'

'Not the way I do it,' Tubs smirked. 'I'll even cut out the steps if I can get away with it.'

The Swifts kicked a ball around aimlessly, much like they did in matches, while they

waited for the Saturday morning practice session to start. They certainly weren't going to exert themselves before their coach, captain and player-manager cajoled them into any purposeful action.

It was ten minutes before Luke, the holder of all these titles, eventually came out of the cabin with Sean trailing some way behind him. It had needed all Luke's powers of persuasion, promises, praise and pandering to Sean's ego before their stylish, left-footed midfielder grudgingly accepted his explanation that what happened had been accidental.

'Got it sorted, have you, Skipper?' Tubs laughed.

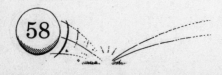

'Yeah, just a misunderstanding,' Luke claimed. 'We've shook hands on it now.'

'Trust you washed them first!' grinned Big Ben.

The session finally got under way and Luke did his best to inspire his depleted group of players to make the necessary effort. He almost took it for granted that not everybody would turn up. There were always a few missing, giving ever more fanciful excuses for their unavoidable absence.

'Big game here, tomorrow, men. We beat the Zebras away, remember – our first win of the season – and we need all three points again . . .'

Luke rarely managed to get through more than a couple of sentences before he was interrupted.

'What time's kick-off?' asked Sanjay.

'Half-past ten.'

'Can't we put it back a bit? Y'know, till the afternoon like some games.'

'We can't suddenly go changing things at the last minute,' Luke told him. 'Why do you want it later, anyway?'

'Got a big family get-together tonight. Could go on for ages.'

'Can't you tell them you need an early night?'

'It'll be too noisy. I wouldn't be able to get to sleep in any case.'

Luke sighed, wondering – not for the first time that season – why things were never simple. 'Just make sure you're here on time, Sanjay, OK? You were brilliant against the Zebras in that first game . . .'

'Yeah, at both ends!' put in Tubs. 'I'll never forget that header of yours.'

'Or the penalty save,' added Gary. 'Well wicked!'

'Right, you see how much we need you, Sanjay,' Luke continued, piling on the flattery. 'We beat this lot once, and we can do it again – but not without you.'

Sanjay lapped up the unaccustomed praise. 'Do my best, Skipper,' he beamed. 'Always do, you know that.'

'Could have fooled us,' murmured Big Ben, thinking of Sanjay's many howlers over the course of the season.

Sanjay was on top form during the brief session of attack versus defence that followed, keeping out goalbound shots from Brain, Gregg and Luke himself, much to the skipper's annoyance. It would have been a rare success for Luke, even in practice. Sanjay only let two goals in, a skimmer from Brain that eluded his grasp and

60

then an unintentional back-header from one of his own defenders that dropped underneath the crossbar.

'Just make sure you don't do one of them tomorrow, Big Ben,' Sanjay complained. 'Have enough problems with the opposition trying to get the ball past me, never mind all the own goal efforts from you-know-who.'

Big Ben grinned. 'You gonna be here, then, are you?'

'Course I am. You ain't got a chance without me around.'

It looked as if Sanjay's boast was going to be put to the test. The Swifts were sitting in the cabin,

already changed – or at least the ten players that had shown up – but there was still no sign of the goalkeeper.

'Can't keep the Zebras waiting any longer,' Luke decided. 'They're all out on the pitch, warming up.'

The skipper held up the team's spare goalie top. 'Er . . . any volunteers?'

'Tubs could go in goal, Skipper,' Gary suggested playfully. 'He'd fill most of it.'

Luke might have guessed there would be no serious takers. 'Right, then,' he said. 'Skipper's duty in a crisis. I'll wear it myself.'

It wasn't the first time that season Luke had been called into action as a stop-gap keeper. His technique tended to be more about gaps than stops, but he hadn't fared quite as badly as others feared. Apart from adding a few more embarrassing, if quite ingenious, own goals to his total, that is.

'Hey! Look!' cried one of the Zebras in delight as a green-clad Luke emerged from the cabin. 'That crazy Asian kid ain't in goal.'

'Magic! That gives us a better chance of beating them this time.'

'Dunno, maybe this kid's even better.'

'Doubt it. He's that weird captain of theirs. Don't reckon he could stop a bus.'

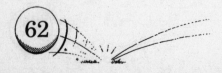

'Well, we'll soon see. Let's test him out early.'

The visitors did exactly that. The black and white striped Zebras, playing in an identical kit to that of the Comp, quickly capitalized on their double advantage of having an extra player on the pitch – and also of having Luke as the opposing keeper.

They swept straight through the middle and their centre-forward tried his luck with a shot from well outside the penalty area. Luke's dive was a textbook effort, but perhaps two pages of his manual on goalkeeping had stuck together – the bit about getting in the way of the ball seemed to have been overlooked. He had an

aerial view of the ball, too, as it passed beneath him, but his despairing glance backwards on landing showed him that it had also skidded wide of the post.

'Phew!' he sighed in relief. 'That was a close thing.'

Luke entrusted the goal-kick to the power of Tubs's mighty hoof, but he was called into action again immediately. With Tubs still out of position, the Zebras left-winger made the most of the huge amount of space that he now enjoyed as he dribbled goalwards. Confused by all the options available to him, the winger hit a hopeful centre-cum-shot that sailed beyond his team-mates and swirled towards the top left-hand corner of Luke's goal.

To his credit, Luke made a valiant effort to save it, but even the taller Sanjay would have been at full stretch to try and reach the ball. To his debit, however, when the ball ricocheted down from the angle of post and bar, Luke was still grounded and only succeeded in fumbling the ball over the line.

'Unlucky, Skipper!' cried Mark generously.

'Yeah, that just about sums me up,' he muttered under his breath. 'Unlucky Luke!'

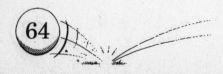

6 Ups and Downs

'Look! Here's Sanjay!' whooped Gary, pointing towards the car park.

Luke had sent Uncle Ray on an urgent errand of mercy to fetch Sanjay, even if the goalie had to be dragged out of bed. Fortunately, Sanjay was already in his goalie kit, not his pyjamas, and had been halfway to the ground when Ray screeched to a halt to give him a lift.

'Soz, overslept,' Sanjay called out. 'What's the score?'

'Losing 5–0!' Tubs bellowed back.

'What! You can't be – I'm not that late. Even Luke hasn't had time to let five in yet.'

'Course I haven't,' Luke protested. 'It's only two.'

It was doubtful whether even Sanjay and Luke together would have prevented the second goal, a rasping close-range volley that tested how firmly the net pegs had been stuck in the soil.

Seeing Sanjay waiting impatiently to come on, the Zebras tried their best to keep the ball in play. They put together a long string of passes before the ball was teed up for the burly centre-forward to whack it goalwards. His arm was already raised in celebration when a green blur dived across his line of vision and turned the ball round the post.

'Great save!' yelled Mark.

'Wicked, Skipper!' grinned Dazza. 'Didn't know you had it in you.'

It was so rare for Luke to do something right on the football pitch that he appeared to forget all about Sanjay until the referee broke the spell.

'Well, are you going to bring on your other keeper or not?' he asked before allowing the corner to be taken. 'He's going bananas on the touchline.'

'Oh, yeah, right – suppose so,' Luke mumbled in a daze. He waved Sanjay on and somewhat reluctantly started to peel off the keeper's top to reveal his gold number nine shirt under-neath.

The Swifts nearly conceded another goal straightaway. The corner was met by a soaring header and the ball clunked against the crossbar with a bang as loud as the farmer's bird-scarer device in the neighbouring field.

'. . . *That could be the turning point of the game,*' burbled the running – well, jogging – commentary as Luke traipsed upfield, feeling cold without his fleece-lined goalie top. *'Now that the Swifts are up to full-strength, there's every chance they can put the Zebras to flight . . .'*

There was indeed a definite shift in the balance of play. The Zebras lost their previous edge of confidence with the arrival of Sanjay, the scourge of their first encounter, and the Swifts hopes grew as they began to enjoy more possession in their opponents' half.

'Huh! Could have stayed in bed and caught up with my beauty sleep,' Sanjay grunted to himself. 'I've hardly touched the ball.'

Chances to score came and went, as they usually did, with Gregg guilty of the worst miss when he blazed over the bar from only two metres out. Just before half-time, however, the Swifts finally gained some reward for their efforts. Brain received a pass from Titch as he cut in from the wing, dribbled past a token challenge and steered the ball into the corner of the net.

'. . . *only 2–1 down now, and the Swifts are in with a good shout . . .*' burbled the match summary as the referee blew for the interval. '*After a few well-chosen words of inspiration from their player-manager during the break, they should be able to take this game by the scruff of the neck and . . .*'

Luke was suddenly yanked back by his shirt collar. 'Just shut it, you!' snarled the Zebras captain. 'I've had just about as much as I can

stand of your voice. If I hear one more peep out of you in the second half, you'll get my size seven boot right up your inbuilt microphone – got it?'

Luke nodded and moved away to a safe distance before risking a retort – and even then the sound was turned right down low. *'Peep!'*

Luke put down his favourite red pen on the desk and gazed at the page of his black notebook with quiet satisfaction. It was filled with his neat, small handwriting, portraying the events of the morning's game against the Zebras.

'Not bad,' he murmured. 'Not bad at all, even though I say so myself.'

He was the only one who was going to say so. Not only because nobody else was allowed access to his private soccer diary, but also because it would be very unlikely for them to form the same opinion as to the quality of its prose. The writer did rather have a tendency to exaggerate the importance of his own role, glossing over any self-inflicted wounds.

Having described his goalkeeping exploits in lurid detail, Luke read over the final paragraphs again, basking in the reflected glory.

The Swifts responded to their coach's half-time tactical talk and took his wise words to heart. Sweeper Ricardo Fortuna, their Italian import who was playing the last game of his loan spell in England, was given licence to Rome (geddit?) further forward and created the equalizer. He exchanged passes cleverly with the skipper in midfield before setting up a chance that even Dazza could not miss.

While the Swifts might have been tempted to settle for a draw, the player-manager drove them on in the quest for all three points in their battle against relegation. 'One point wouldn't have been enough,' Luke Crawford told reporters after the match. 'We had to throw caution to the wind.'

This brave policy almost backfired when Sanjay was left exposed and raced off his line to save at an attacker's feet, but earned its reward a few minutes from the end. Ricki gave the Swifts a farewell present worth his weight in gold – or certainly in lira – when he stormed upfield to meet a cross and head the ball home. This gave the Swifts the double over the Zebras, winning both league encounters 3–2.

'Survival is now in our own hands,' said the skipper confidently. 'We won't go down without a fight.'

Luke stood up and paced the room in restless excitement. 'Two crunch games coming up,' he said aloud. 'What a way to end the season!'

Luke wasn't yet sure what part, if any, he might yet play in the first encounter, the Comp's Cup Final next Saturday morning. Frosty still hadn't named his team, but Luke remained hopeful he might be included. Like the Swifts, Frosty did not exactly have the luxury of a large squad to choose from.

'Be nice to win a medal,' Luke murmured dreamily and then broke out of his reverie. 'But it'd mean nothing if the Swifts went and got relegated next day. Can't let that happen – we just can't – not now . . .'

Big Ben's clearance upfield was punted too far ahead of the strikers and the ball bounced harmlessly out of play for a goal-kick.

'What kind of a pass was that meant to be?' complained Gregg. 'I'm not a greyhound, y'know.'

Big Ben grinned. 'No, but I reckoned the baby elephant in goal needed some exercise!'

Frosty let out a heavy sigh as he watched Tubs waddle after the ball. He guessed that the boy had only volunteered to have a go between the posts in this after-school practice to save doing any more running about.

'Anything wrong, sir?' came a voice behind him.

Frosty turned and gazed at Gary without apparent recognition.

'Um . . . it's just that you sounded a bit . . . like, fed up, sir, you know . . .'

'*Fed up?* I've been fed up for about the past twenty years,' the teacher growled as it began to drizzle. 'Fed up of being rained on, snowed on, blown about and half frozen to death – all for the sake of school sport.'

Gary glanced round, hoping that somebody might come and rescue him from such a torrent of self-pity. He was alone. To his credit, he attempted to fill the embarrassed silence between them.

'I'm sure it's not been all bad, sir,' he began, 'I mean, your teams must have won a few cups over the years – and we're in the Final on Saturday.'

'Oh, yes, how could I forget that?' Frosty retorted. 'I'm really looking forward to another public humiliation against Grimthorpe.'

At that very moment, Luke came trundling by, trying to dribble a ball. He found the triple combination of moving, ball control and commentating on his actions all too much. He stumbled over the ball and fell flat on his face.

Frosty caught Gary's eye and waved a dismissive arm around at the scene in general. 'It's Fate's last chance to kick old Frosty in the teeth,' he muttered, 'or at least what he's got left after grinding them all these years.'

Gary was so taken aback by Frosty using his own nickname that he almost missed the significance of the teacher's choice of words. 'Um . . . *last* chance, sir?' he repeated.

'Yes, last chance, boy,' he nodded, not even bothering to try and evade the issue. 'You might as well know. I was going to tell you all, anyway, after the Final. There seems to be a rumour

going round the school already, so it might as well be out in the open.'

'What's that, sir?' asked Gary, feigning innocence.

'I'm packing up at the end of term.'

Gary tried to look more shocked than pleased. 'Are you going to another school?'

'No, thank goodness. It's bad enough here. I'm retiring,' he admitted and then added, 'and that's *early* retirement I'm talking about, boy. I'm getting out while I've still got all my marbles left – and some of my hair!'

The rain started to come down harder. 'Right, you lot, we're going in,' Frosty shouted, pointing towards the school. 'I've had enough.'

7 Fire!

April was living up to its reputation for showers and the wind chill ensured that the temperature felt more like February. The weather was so bad that Luke was the only one who bothered to turn up at the rainswept recky for the Swifts midweek training session and even he stayed inside the changing cabin.

The skipper kept himself warm with an old single-bar electric fire and a solo game of football, using a tennis ball and one of the benches as a goal. Accompanied by his wild commentary, his frenetic, unco-ordinated actions were not a pretty sight – or sound – but no-one else was around to complain. This was doubly fortunate,

both for them and for him, as there were no witnesses as to who had broken the small pane of glass over the door.

Luke also found himself alone outside the school gates on Saturday morning, waiting to travel into the nearby town of Padley – the neutral venue for the Cup Final. Underneath his tracksuit and coat, Luke was wearing the black and white number thirteen shirt thrown to him (or at him) the previous day at the team meeting as the Comp's only available substitute.

'Might even give you that shirt as a farewell present,' Frosty had remarked gruffly, though with a little glint in his eye. 'Must be like an old friend to you by now.'

It was some while before anybody else showed up at the gates and Luke was relieved to see the Garner twins. He was beginning to think Frosty might have played some cruel joke on him and secretly arranged for the other players to gather somewhere else instead.

'Been here long, Luke?' asked Gregg, reserving his title of Skipper for Sundays.

'Bet he camped out all night,' chuckled Gary. 'Just to make sure we didn't leave without him.'

Luke took the usual banter in good heart. 'At least it's not raining yet this morning,' he said.

'Give it time,' muttered Mr Garner, eyeing the dark clouds overhead suspiciously.

Tubs was the next one to appear on the scene. His arrival was unexpected in the sense that he was running – or at least the nearest that Tubs would ever get to that unfamiliar form of locomotion. He rarely broke into anything more than a trot in an actual game.

'Hey! What's got into you, Tubs?' Gregg shouted. 'Where's the fire?'

It was some while before Tubs was in any state to answer. He looked shocked as well as out of breath. 'At the . . . recky!' he gasped, heaving.

'What d'yer mean, at the recky? What is?'

'The fire . . . you idiot!'

'What fire?' demanded Luke, suddenly concerned.

'The fire . . . that burnt down . . . the cabin!' Tubs managed to choke out.

Luke's cheeks, reddened by the wind, turned ghastly white as the blood drained from his face. 'Our cabin? Is this some kind of stupid joke?'

All of Tubs' spare flesh wobbled about as he vigorously shook his head in denial. 'Straight up . . . Luke . . .' he replied. 'Took a short cut . . . through the recky . . . to get here . . . and there it was . . . or wasn't. It's gone!'

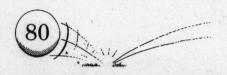

'What! The cabin?'

'Yes! Are you deaf . . . as well as daft?' Tubs panted. 'Watch my lips – cabin is no more. Kaput – got it? All that's left are the front steps!'

Luke didn't take in very much of the first half. Not because the crowd was so great that he could barely get a view of the action – he could have stretched out along the touchline anywhere he liked – but because his mind kept drifting back to the recky.

Terrible pangs of guilt stabbed at Luke's conscience as he pictured the scene of devastation. 'Sure I switched that electric fire off when I left on Thursday,' he murmured to himself. 'Must have done.'

'Sorry I'm late,' said Dad, suddenly appearing at Luke's side and turning up his coat collar against the rain that was starting. 'Only I got called to the recky by the police. Guess you've already heard the bad news?'

He didn't need an answer. Luke's miserable face said it all.

'Cabin's totally gutted, I'm afraid,' Dad told him. 'Everything inside has been lost – nets, balls, the lot. Good job the posts were already set up on the pitch or they would've been barbecued too.'

'Um . . . how do they think it happened?' asked Luke hesitantly.

'They reckon it was vandals. I'd just like to get my hands on them, whoever they are.'

Luke gulped. 'What are we going to do about tomorrow's match?'

'Have to speak to Ray first. League rules say we must have nets on the posts for one thing – and a ball might perhaps come in useful too.'

Dad paused and nodded towards the pitch. 'What's the score here, then?' he asked. 'Have I missed much?'

Luke shrugged. 'Dunno – not really been watching.'

Dad was flabbergasted. 'Blimey! Things must be bad!' he gasped. 'If you can't keep track of how many Sanjay's let in, nobody can.'

At that moment, Jon received a pass on the halfway line and the next Grimthorpe player to touch the ball was the goalkeeper as he picked it out of the netting. Jon had treated the spectators to their first real glimpse of his special talents, taking the ball on a mazy run past several red shirts before chipping it teasingly over the advancing keeper.

'Great goal by our Jon, eh?' beamed Ray, trotting up to his brother. 'We're only 3–1 down now. That's really set the game alight . . .'

Ray realized what he'd just said and gave a little apologetic smile. 'Well, perhaps not the best way to put it in the circumstances.'

Luke sighed. Nobody would ever describe anything he did on the pitch in such glowing terms. Off the pitch, well, that was another matter . . .

'Luke! Luke!' came a shout. 'You're on.'

Luke was jolted out of his dark thoughts. He hadn't even bothered to go and join his teammates to receive Frosty's half-time tongue-lashing. He knew the teacher would at best ignore him or, at worst, insult him and he could do without suffering either indignity right now.

'C'mon, Luke!' Jon called out again. 'Get that coat off.'

Perhaps for the first time in his life – at least, ever since he'd been able to stand up – Luke wasn't in the mood for playing football. 'Typical!' he grunted. 'Trust old Frosty to go and make things even worse for me.'

'Good luck,' said Dad. 'Glad I got here in time to see you play. Go and show 'em how to do it.'

Luke forced a smile. He could *tell* them how something should be done all right, but even his dad knew there was no way in the world he could actually *show* them. He'd leave any practical

demonstrations to his cousin.

Frosty had already given up the game as lost and, to the captain's amazement, made no objection to Jon's suggestion that Luke might come on as an extra attacker.

Normally, Luke's natural enthusiasm would have over-ridden any instructions to stay in position and caused him to pop up in the unlikeliest of places. On this occasion, however, his heart simply wasn't in it. When the Comp were defending a corner early in the second half, he stood idly in the centre-circle with Gregg, their presence at least obliging Grimthorpe to keep players back to cover them.

'Are you OK, Luke?' asked Gregg. 'I mean, you're not even droning on as usual. What's the matter?'

'It's the cabin,' he murmured. 'It's been a bit of a shock.'

'Yeah, right. Do you think we'll still be able to play tomorrow?'

'Only if we can get hold of some nets in time.'

Gregg thought for a moment, watching Tubs slice the ball out for yet another corner. 'What about Frosty?' he suggested. 'You could ask him if we might borrow some from the school.'

'He'd never let us do that.'

Gregg gave a shrug. 'No harm in asking. He can only say no.'

'Yeah, and that's exactly what he'd delight in doing as well. Bet he wouldn't even give me the mud off his boots.'

'Perhaps if you caught him in a good mood?'

Luke gave a snort. 'No chance! Have *you* ever seen Frosty in a good mood? And he sure won't be today, getting stuffed in the Final.'

'Wake up, you dozy pair!'

The Comp's new strike force were so busy talking, they didn't realize the ball had been booted away until Frosty's bellow stirred them into belated action. Gregg managed to get in a challenge, blocking the attempted clearance, and the ball spun across to Luke. He shaped to knock a pass back to Jon, but made no contact and the ball slithered through his legs.

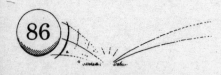

It was a perfect dummy! His marker was completely fooled, thrown off-balance, and was unable to stop the ball running free towards the wing. Brain had sprinted upfield and found himself with a clear route to goal.

The Grimthorpe keeper came out to meet the winger in the vain hope of forcing an error, but with Brain's two-footed ball-skills, there would only be one winner in this type of situation. Brain waltzed round the stranded goalie and tucked the ball into the empty net before dribbling it back to the centre-circle so as not to delay the restart.

'Magic, Brain!' Jon congratulated the scorer. 'We're only one goal behind now. We can still win this.'

Brain grinned. 'You're starting to sound like Luke.'

'Sorry, must be 'cos I'm captain,' Jon said sheepishly. 'Didn't used to care much who won so long as it was a good game.'

'I'll let you off. It *is* the Final after all. Wouldn't mind winning the Cup myself.'

'OK, then – let's do it!'

8 The Swinging Pendulum

'C'mon, Reds!' cried the Grimthorpe teacher. 'Sort it out!'

His players were slow to recognize the danger signs of the Comp's revival. If the Reds had been assuming they already had one hand on the trophy, their grip was first loosened and then prized off altogether.

The Comp went close to levelling the scores twice before Brain moved smoothly on to Jon's pin-point pass and slid the ball underneath the goalie's dive for the equalizer. Jon and Brain were the team's genuine stars, capable – when on song – of forcing any opponents to dance to their tune.

'Great stuff!' cried Luke, pushing his worries to the back of his mind during the goal celebrations. 'We've got 'em on the run!'

Frosty was astonished by such a recovery. He had given the game up as dead at half-time. 'Keep it up!' he called out. 'You can win this.'

The players already knew that. Only rarely now did the ball come Sanjay's way and stir the keeper into action. He comfortably held on to a hopeful, long-range effort and then had to deal with a back-pass from Big Ben. He picked the ball up and prepared to boot it as far as he could . . .

When the whistle blew, Sanjay thought it was the signal for the end of the match and he belted the ball high into the air instead. Only then did he realize that something was wrong – terribly wrong. He was helped to arrive at this conclusion by all the abuse he was receiving from his teammates.

'Handball!' announced the referee. 'Free-kick to the Reds.'

'You idiot, Sanjay!' cried Gary. 'What did you go and do a stupid thing like that for? You know you can't handle the ball from a back-pass!'

Sanjay shook his head in dismay. 'Soz – I just wasn't thinking, like . . .'

His voice trailed away. The Comp players were in no mood for explanations or apologies.

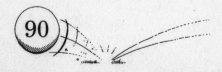

'Make a wall!' ordered Jon.

Luke was about to join it when his cousin grabbed him by the arm. 'You go upfield, Luke,' Jon urged. 'We need a target man in case we make a quick breakaway.'

'Good thinking, Johan,' grinned Luke. It didn't cross his mind that Jon might simply want him out of the way.

Luke's presence didn't cause the Reds any particular concern. 'I'll look after this clown,' announced the centre-back, waving his fellow defenders forward to join the attack. 'He's no bother.'

Luke ignored the comment and gave the unemployed commentator his job back. *'Here we*

are, right near the end of the Cup Final, and the Comp have some desperate defending to do. The human wall prepares to risk life and limb to block this free-kick as it looks like it's gonna be a real blaster. The kicker runs in and lets fly . . . Oh! That must have hurt Tubs, the biggest brick in the wall. And now the ball's been hoofed clear and . . .'

'Luke!' came Jon's cry, cutting across the commentary. 'Chase it!'

Luke jolted into belated action. He scurried after the ball and managed to reach it just ahead of the slow-moving opponent, receiving a kick on the ankle as his reward. He stumbled and lost what little control he had over the ball, but as his marker was about to hammer it back into the Comp's half, Luke stretched out a leg and toe-poked it away. The defender whacked into Luke's foot instead and the pair of them collapsed to the ground in pain.

Luke didn't even see the goal, preventing any live commentary on how Jon gained possession of the loose ball and then lobbed it calmly over the keeper's head. The first Luke knew about what had happened was when he was suddenly hauled to his feet and nearly deafened.

'4–3!' Gregg shrieked into his ear. 'We've won the Cup!'

*

92

'So where did you get the nets?' asked Big Ben.

'From the Comp,' Luke replied, watching his dad and uncle fasten the nets on to the goalposts at the far end of the recreation ground.

'Did you go and pinch 'em or something?'

'Course not. Just asked Frosty if the Swifts could borrow some nets for our last league match and he said yes. Even lent us a couple of footballs.'

'Amazing!' Big Ben chuckled. 'Perhaps he *is* human after all!'

'Well, we *had* just won the cup for him,' said Luke, fingering the medal that still hung around his neck on a coloured ribbon. It was the first medal Luke had ever received. Not just at football, but for anything.

He was feeling a great sense of relief now, knowing that he wasn't to blame for the cabin fire. When the footballers returned to Swillsby after the Final, they learnt that the arsonists had also damaged several other buildings, including a barn, part of the village hall and the old scout hut.

'Er, just one more thing, Skipper,' said Big Ben, grinning. 'Are you gonna be wearing that all match?'

'What?'

'That medal. Bet you even slept with it round your neck!'

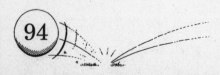

'Course not,' Luke replied, reddening. 'What d'yer think I am?'

The defender didn't like to say. Nor did he see Luke slip the medal inside his soccer shirt out of sight as more of the team began to arrive.

'Just for safe keeping,' Luke told himself. 'I mean, can't leave it lying around anywhere, can I? Somebody might nick it.'

The players stood about at first, not knowing quite what to do in the absence of the cabin.

'So where are we gonna change?' asked Sean.

'Alfresco,' said Luke.

'Where's that?'

'Here.'

'Where?'

'It means outside,' Luke explained. 'Ricki told me it comes from the Italian originally.'

'Pity he had to go back to Italy himself today,' muttered Tubs. 'We needed him here.'

Sean wouldn't let the matter drop. 'You mean, we've all got to strip off in the open where everybody can see us?'

'Everybody!' Titch cackled, looking around comically at the otherwise deserted recky. 'Don't seem as if the prospect of watching us lot parading around in our Y-fronts has drawn much of a crowd!'

'The Rangers won't like it,' Sean muttered, taking off his coat.

'Well, they'll just have to lump it, won't they?' said Luke, losing his patience. 'What else can we do?'

'Shame it's not foggy like last time,' put in Mark. 'Even Tubs could have streaked across the pitch then and nobody would have noticed!'

The Swifts' previous attempt to play this fixture against Padley Park Rangers had been abandoned in the fog with the game officially goal-less, despite Luke's claims that he'd scored just before the referee called a halt. The visibility by that time was so poor that not even the

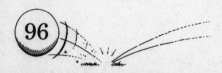

Rangers keeper saw him put the ball in the net.

Sean was correct about one thing. The visitors certainly didn't think much of the situation when they eventually rolled up and had to change, grumbling, in the car park.

'Right, men – all ready?' cried Luke to get his teammates attention. Nobody responded to his usual rallying call, but he carried on regardless. 'One last big effort today and the Swifts will be safe.'

'Are you sure about that, Skipper?' said Titch. 'I mean, we ain't got many points this season.'

'Nor have the Wanderers. So long as we win today, we'll be OK.'

'What if we don't?'

'Look, like I've told you, it's between us and Wanderers who goes down – right?' Luke explained, deciding to spell out the situation again. 'We're both playing our last game today and we're one point ahead of them. So if we pick up the three points for a win, they can't catch us.'

'But what if we don't?' Titch persisted, repeating his question.

'Well, in that case, it'll depend how they get on, won't it?'

'And how we gonna know that? They gonna show the results on the telly, are they?'

'No need. Dad's got a mobile phone.'

'So?'

'And so has Uncle Ray.'

'Fat lot of good that is,' chortled Tubs, gazing over at the two men who had just finished dealing with the nets. 'May as well save the cost of a call. They're standing next to each other.'

Luke pulled a face. 'They won't be in a bit. Ray's taking Johan to watch the Wanderers game and they're going to ring to let us know what's happening.'

'Ah, the wonders of modern technology!' put in Big Ben sarcastically. 'I trust they know how to work the things.'

'Course they do,' Luke scoffed, trying to hide his own doubts.'

Ray saw the first goal go in even before he left the recky, but it didn't send him off in an optimistic mood. It was scored by the Rangers.

For once, it was not due to any mistake of Luke's, or even Sanjay's. It was simply a very good goal, rounding off a move that would have tested the best defence in the league – and that was something the Swifts certainly could not boast.

Their *goals against* tally almost needed a separate column in the league table, the number

was so big. It was no use them hoping to stay up on *goal difference*. If they finished level on points with Wanderers, the Swifts were doomed for relegation into the new bottom division that was being formed for all the clubs wanting to join the league next season.

The Rangers kept Sanjay very busy for the next quarter of an hour, but they only succeeded in playing the unpredictable goalie into form. He produced a series of excellent saves, the best being a spectacular leap to pluck the ball out of the air. He even clung on to it as he hit the ground.

By contrast, the Rangers keeper had been largely idle and he was caught napping by a surprise Swifts raid up the right wing. Dazza's speed took him past a defender and his centre-cum-shot found the keeper out of position. The boy's blushes were only spared when the ball dipped a fraction too late and clipped the top of the crossbar on its way out for a goal-kick.

That should have served as a sufficient wake-up alarm call, but when Brain broke through a few minutes later, the keeper was again in no-man's-land. Brain's cross sailed over his head and dropped perfectly on to Gregg's. Even then, Gregg almost steered the ball wide of the target,

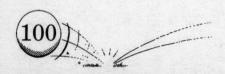

but it snicked the inside of the post and deflected into the netting.

'The equalizer!' cried Luke, rushing over to congratulate both the scorer and the provider. 'There's no stopping us now.'

9 Keep in Touch

The phone rang almost as soon as the Swifts gathered together at half-time. Luke's dad jabbed at a button and put the mobile to his ear.

'Hello,' he said. 'Who's that?'

'It's me, you fool,' came his brother's response. *'Who d'yer think?'*

'Oh, right, sorry – so what's the news?'

'Bad. Wanderers went 2–1 in front just before the break. What about the Swifts?'

'Better. Everything still to play for here. Gregg's just equalized. What shall I tell the kids?'

'Tell them the truth,' said Ray. *'No good trying to mislead them, that's only asking for trouble.'*

'Right, OK, leave it to me.'

Dad switched off and faced a clamour of voices wanting to know what was happening in the other game.

'C'mon, Dad – don't keep us in suspense,' Luke pleaded.

Dad made an instant decision to apply a bit of amateur psychology. 'Good news,' he announced, forcing a smile to cover his deception. He didn't want the players to be discouraged by the truth. 'Wanderers are losing.'

'Heavily?' Luke said hopefully.

'Er . . . no, just a goal in it at half-time.'

Luke eyed his dad suspiciously. 'So why did you have to ask Ray what to tell us?'

'Well, he said the Wanderers were still look-ing dangerous, that's all,' Dad replied, a little flustered. 'We can't afford to relax.'

'No way we'll do that,' Luke asserted. 'As long as we win, they won't be able to catch us.'

'Right, you heard your captain, lads,' Dad said. 'Just concentrate on your own job. Win this game and we're safe, it's as simple as that.'

'Huh! Winning's never as simple as that for us,' muttered Big Ben.

'Yeah, but if Wanderers *do* lose, it won't matter if we do, too, will it?' Gary pointed out. 'We'll still be OK.'

'You can't rely on that,' Dad said quickly. 'Just go and do your best, lads, that's all we can ask of you. Good luck!'

'Reckon we're gonna need it,' muttered Sanjay, watching the animated discussions in the opposing camp thirty metres away. 'Bet they can't work out why they're not already well ahead.'

'It's thanks to you, Sanjay,' Luke chirped, pleased to have the rare chance to praise his goalie. 'Keep playing like that and there's no way they'll get the ball past you again.'

That was asking for trouble. Luke should have known better. Sanjay's form was as changeable

as the weather in an English summer. One minute glorious sunshine, the next a downpour of rain – with always the risk of occasional showers.

Five minutes into the second half, Sanjay dropped the inevitable clanger – and the ball – and his teammates felt like reaching for the shelter of their umbrellas. Having done well to turn the original shot around the post, he let the corner slip through his hands and a lurking striker knocked the loose ball between two defenders on the line to put Rangers back in front.

Dad's phone went once more. It was Jon this time.

''Fraid Wanderers have scored again,' he reported. *'They're 3–1 up now. What's the score your end?'*

'Not looking good. We've just gone 2–1 down.'

'Pity! Well, make sure Luke knows about Wanderers, won't you?'

'Sure, thanks for telling me.'

Luke came running over. 'Heard the phone. Wanderers haven't equalized, have they?'

Dad shook his head. 'Er . . . no,' he said, attempting an answer which was strictly true, if not exactly accurate. 'Just you keep your mind on the game here, that's the main thing.'

Luke veered away to broadcast the latest news to the world via his commentary and then to his teammates. 'Big effort, men,' he cried, shaking his fists. 'C'mon, we can still do it.'

'Just hope things work out OK,' Dad muttered, 'or I'm in big trouble!'

His hopes were raised a minute later when Brain was gifted a great chance to put the Swifts back on level terms. A Rangers defender turned the ball back towards his keeper without noticing Brain was hovering. The winger reached the ball first and pushed it wide of the onrushing keeper, but unfortunately just wide of the goal too.

Brain stared after it in horror. 'Can't believe I missed that!' he groaned.

Nor could Luke. And nor could he believe the arrival of a most unexpected spectator. 'What's *he* doing here?' he muttered. 'I hope he's not gonna bring us bad luck.'

Frosty wandered up to stand next to Luke's dad. 'Hello again,' the teacher greeted him. 'What's the damage?'

'Damage?' repeated Dad, as much taken aback as the players. 'Er . . . to the cabin, you mean?'

Frosty gazed over to the charred wreckage. It made a sorry sight. 'No, I can see that for myself,' he replied. 'I meant, how many are your Swifts losing by today?'

'Oh, sorry. Well, not doing badly, I suppose – only 2–1 down, but we really need to win.'

'So I gather – bit much to hope for, isn't it?'

Dad took offence. 'Well, they managed it for you yesterday.'

Frosty nodded slowly. 'Aye, they did that,' he acknowledged, but couldn't resist a little dig. 'Shame Jon can't turn out for you as well, though.'

'He's doing his bit – keeping us in touch with the other vital game . . .'

The phone rang again at that moment.

'Excuse me,' Dad said, clamping it to his ear.

Jon relayed his report and Dad muttered a brief response, not wishing to become involved in any long explanation with Frosty nearby.

'So what's the situation there, then?' Frosty asked.

Dad hesitated, but he couldn't bring himself to lie to the teacher as well. 'Wanderers have just let a goal in, but they're still winning unfortunately . . .'

'Do these lads know that?'

'Well, you see, actually I was . . .'

Frosty took matters into his own hands. 'C'mon, you Swifts, pull your fingers out!' he roared. 'No good losing when the other lot are winning.'

The Swifts glanced at one another, startled. 'What's he mean, they're winning?' muttered Big Ben. 'Can't be.'

'Must have hit back second half,' groaned Mark. 'We're dead!'

Luke ran towards the touchline in alarm. 'What's going on, Dad?' he gasped. 'Tell me.'

'Sorry – Wanderers are 3–2 up,' he admitted reluctantly.

Luke's world caved in. He knew that even a draw wouldn't be enough to save the Swifts now, not if the Wanderers picked up all three points. Instinctively, he put his hand inside his shirt

110

and clasped his medal for comfort. It seemed to inspire him.

'C'mon, men!' he called out, trying to sound positive when he was choked with negative emotions. 'We need to score some goals.'

That was easier said than done. But if cousin Jon couldn't come to the Swifts rescue, then perhaps cousin Ricki would suffice.

'Hey! Look who's here!' cried Gary, pointing at the car park. 'Thought he was flying off to Italy today.'

Ricki galloped towards the pitch. 'Car broke down again,' he shouted out. 'We miss plane.'

'How did you get here?' Luke demanded.

'Laura – her father bring me,' he panted, pulling his boots out of a bag. 'You need me?'

'Sure do,' Luke admitted. 'We have plenty need of you – get 'em on!'

The player-manager decided to gamble by taking off a defender and playing Ricki up front as another attacker. His sweeper role was forgotten.

'Give him your shirt, Mark,' Luke said. 'We don't have a spare one.'

Mark pulled a face. 'So long as he doesn't have to wear my shorts as well. I'm not standing on the recky in my pants.'

'So this is that Ricki kid I've heard about, is it?'

mused Frosty, stroking his stubbly chin. 'Should be interesting to see which Crawford he takes after.'

Ricki's first touch certainly bore the family trademark, but of the Luke variety, ballooning a pass over Brain's head out of play. His second, however, showed he had the potential class of Jon about him as well. He caught the ball on the volley, about knee high, and sent it swerving only centimetres over the Rangers crossbar.

'Hmm, strange combination,' Frosty murmured. 'Got a bit of both in him by the look of it. What a crazy mixed-up kid!'

'Come on, Ricki!' cried Laura. 'Come on the Swifts. You can do it.'

Perhaps Laura had brought them a touch of Lady Luck. In their very next attack, the ball fell at the feet of Ricki in the penalty area. His first effort, a left-foot scoop, was blocked, but he seized on the rebound and hit a right-footed rocket straight at the keeper who parried the ball away to save his teeth. A goalmouth scramble ensued with the ball ricocheting between the bodies until a thin leg poked out of the crush and scuffed it over the line.

Controversy reigned. As the referee signalled a goal, the visitors were appealing for a foul – any kind of foul – claiming pushing, kicking and

shirt-pulling all at once, but the Swifts were much too busy celebrating to notice. Only when the party broke up did it become clear who was claiming the credit as the scorer.

'That's m'boy!' Dad yelled. 'You've shown 'em how to do it!'

Unfortunately, Luke was not able to manage a repeat demonstration. The Rangers decided to settle for a draw and, in the end, the Swifts had to be satisfied with a single point too.

'That's it, there goes the final whistle,' sighed the commentator, still in a bit of a daze after the thrill of scoring. 'Not even the skipper's scrambled equalizer may be enough to save his team. As I hand you back to the studio, their fate now hangs in the balance . . .'

He had to stop talking. His path was barred by the Rangers captain. 'You lot were dead jammy,' the boy sneered. 'We should have thrashed you.'

Luke gave a shrug. He couldn't be bothered to argue. He had more important things on his mind, like the Wanderers result. If their rivals had won, the Swifts would be relegated.

Dad was messing with the mobile as Luke approached, trying to get through to Ray without success.

'Here, let me have a go,' Luke said, holding out his hand impatiently.

As Dad tossed him the phone in frustration, it jangled into life and Luke nearly dropped it into the water bucket. He put it shakily to his ear as his teammates crowded around, expecting to hear the worst.

'Hello, it's Luke here. We drew two each. What's gone on there?'

The audience craned forward, hoping to catch a few words, but all they could hear was a crackle on the line.

'Soz, I didn't catch that, Johan,' said Luke. 'Got some interference. Say again . . . who scored?'

After a few more crackles, Luke suddenly flung the phone up into the air and Dad went scampering after it.

'We've done it!' Luke cried at the top of his voice. 'We're safe!'

The Swifts cheered and jumped all over each other in relief, and it was some while before anyone calmed down enough to ask a sensible question.

'So what exactly went on there, Skipper?' said a half-naked Titch, who had somehow lost his shirt in all the excitement.

'The Wanderers screwed up!' Luke exclaimed.

'Johan said they panicked and threw it away.'

'Just like you did with my phone,' Dad grumbled, giving it a shake.

'What was the score?' Tubs demanded.

'Same as our Cup Final – 4–3! Wanderers went and let in two goals in the last few minutes of the game. They must be pig-sick!'

Luke himself felt totally overcome, mentally and physically drained of emotion. He went to sit on the blackened steps of the burnt-out cabin and let his automatic commentary describe the scene. The visitors were trailing moodily back to the car park, Frosty had already started to

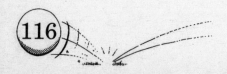

dismantle one of the nets, their Latin Romeo was giving Laura a hug right in front of her father and his dishevelled, delirious teammates were still behaving like lunatics.

'Even after all the recent shocks, the biggest must be that – for once – things have actually worked out right for the Swifts,' Luke murmured as a final summary. *'And you can bet your life that this crazy bunch of unsung heroes will want to do it all over again next season too! Soccer mad, all of 'em – Luke Crawford's Barmy Army!'*

Crawford's Corner

Hi! It's me again, Luke Crawford – still on a high after skippering the Swifts to our dramatic end of season success. Well, at least we didn't finish bottom of the table and that's as good a reason as any to celebrate. Not to mention helping to win the cup for old Frosty in his final year at the Comp of course. Oops! I've just gone and mentioned it.

Was originally thinking of telling you here about a few soccer shocks of the past to go with the title of this book. Like, for instance, when the part-time footballers of the United States beat favourites England 1–0 during the 1950 World Cup – or when an on-loan goalkeeper went upfield for a corner in the dying seconds of a game in 1999 to score the vital goal that saved Carlisle being relegated from the Football League – or even when a referee last dared to give a penalty against Manchester United at Old Trafford!

But I'm too excited right now to go trawling through all my collection of soccer annuals to dig out more examples of such fascinating feats. If you've got time, why don't you do some research of your own into the record books and read about all the amazing things that have happened over the years on the football field? Use the Internet, too, and see what else you can find out.

Instead, I've decided to return to my favourite subject – the legendary superstar, **Johan Cruyff**, known to friends as Jopie, and nicknamed **the Flying Dutchman**. Unbelievably, I still sometimes get blank looks from other kids when I rave on about how great a player he was, the best ever as far as I'm concerned – better even than Pelé. You'd have thought they'd never heard of him! Yeah, OK, I know Johan graced the scene well before our time, but footballers only have short careers at the top. The players you rate now will soon be history.

But what a fabulous history Johan Cruyff has, though, both as a world-famous star player and as a successful coach. In my view, there's no-one to equal his achievements, even though he never managed to win the World Cup. The closest he came to that was as captain of the brilliant Dutch

team which lost 2–1 in the 1974 Final to West Germany. This was despite their exciting style of play, known as *Total Football*, where all the versatile Dutch players constantly switched positions during games.

Speaking of the Net, by the way, there are hundreds of sites on the subject of Johan Cruyff, even if some of them are in Dutch and other languages! (His name rhymes with either *life* or *roof*, whichever you prefer.) Browse through that lot and you'll know nearly as much as I do about his fantastic career. To start you off, here's a potted biography of his life and honours:

- born Hendrik Johannes Cruyff on 25 April 1947 in Amsterdam
- family lived across the street from Ajax stadium
- started playing for Ajax Juniors at age of ten
- won his first cup when he was 14 and played all his later career with that trademark number 14 on the back of his shirt
- 1964 – scored on first team debut for Ajax at 16
- 1966 – scored last-minute equalizer in 2–2 draw on debut for Holland

121

- won three successive European Cups with Ajax – 1971/72/73
- 1973 – transferred to Barcelona for a then record fee of £922,000
- 1974 – birth of son Jordi, later to play also for Ajax, Barcelona and then Manchester United
- won ten league championship medals:
  Ajax – 1966/67/68/70/72/73/82/83
  Barcelona – 1974 (their first for 14 years in his first season there)
  Feyenoord – 1984
- won seven cup-winners medals:
  Ajax – 1967/70/71/72/83
  Barcelona – 1978
  Feyenoord – 1984
- voted European Footballer of the Year in 1971, 1973 & 1974
- voted best European Footballer of the Century in 1999
- retired from international football in 1977 before the '78 World Cup
- played a couple of years in America before returning to Ajax in 1981
- hung up his boots in 1984 after season with rivals Feyenoord

- Ajax technical director, trainer & coach from 1985 to 1988
- Barcelona coach from 1988 to 1996
- main honours as coach:

League Championships: Barcelona –
   1991/92/93/94

Cups: Ajax – 1986/87
       Barcelona – 1990

European Cup: Barcelona – 1992

European Cup-Winners Cups:
   Ajax – 1987
   Barcelona – 1989

- Fired as Barcelona coach in 1996 after dispute with club president
- Celebrated his 50th birthday in 1997 in semi-retirement, but set up the Johan Cruyff Foundation to raise money to help disabled people play sport. Now fully recovered from his earlier heart problems, due to heavy smoking, he may yet be back. Watch this space!

Phew! A record like that, both as player and coach, would take some beating, eh? To repeat what I put in *Soccer Stars* when I was writing about lots of great players, I described Johan Cruyff as the

complete footballer. He had everything: pace, acceleration, instant ball control, amazing balance and superb passing skills – and he also scored loads of goals (netting 33 times in his 48 internationals). He was such an elegant player, so versatile and original, even inventing a new ingenious piece of dribbling trickery which became known as the 'Cruyff Turn'. You must have seen it shown on TV – but I bet you can't do it! (No, neither can I, sadly.)

I don't want to make out that Johan was a saint of course. Far from it. He was quite a controversial figure, on and off the field. He knew exactly what he wanted and was always prepared to argue his case. He was even booked at half-time in the 1974 World Cup Final for questioning the referee about his decisions as they left the pitch! He was also the first Dutch player to be sent off in an international and received a year's ban!

Some people might have viewed him as arrogant at times, but not by those who really knew him. He had to put up with a lot of rough treatment in matches, and did so with dignity and self-control, even though many defenders weren't quick enough to foul him. Before they realized what he was going to do, he'd done it and whipped past them. He had

tremendous speed off the mark and was able to do things naturally that most other players could never do after years of practice. That's what made him so special. He may have been frail looking, but he had great stamina, technique and tactical knowledge. He worked hard to overcome any weaknesses in his game, building up the power in his left foot, for example, by training with weights on his ankle in his teens to develop more strength so that he could kick a ball equally hard with both feet.

As a coach, he stressed what he had always believed as a player – that simple play is the most beautiful, and that you should try and play in an attacking style to make the game a more enjoyable spectacle to watch. He once said that if a team is 4–0 ahead near the end of a match, it's better for the next shot to hit the woodwork rather than go in so the crowd could 'oooh' and 'aaah' in excitement.

Football, he insisted, is a game you play with your brains. There's no need to run around so much. You just have to be in the right place at the right time, not too early, not too late. (Tubs would obviously agree with him there – trouble is, Tubs can't run even if he wanted to and he hasn't got

many brains either! Only joking, Tubs, my old mate, if you happen to read this.)

Right, so there you are. Better stop or I'll go on all day and I'm getting hungry. But now you know why Johan Cruyff was such a magnificent footballer and top class coach. No excuse any more to say 'Who?' when you hear his name. He WAS and ALWAYS WILL BE the GREATEST! 'That's logical,' as J.C. himself often liked to say to clinch an argument.

See ya!

Luke

ABOUT THE AUTHOR

Rob Childs was born and grew up in Derby. His childhood ambition was to become an England cricketer or footballer – preferably both! After university, however, he went into teaching and taught in primary and high schools in Leicestershire, where he now lives. Always interested in school sports, he coached school teams and clubs across a range of sports, and ran area representative teams in football, cricket and athletics.

Recognizing a need for sports fiction for young readers, he decided to have a go at writing such stories himself and now has more than fifty books to his name, including the popular *The Big Match* series, published by Young Corgi Books and the *County Cup* series.

Rob has now left teaching in order to be able to write full-time. Married to Joy, a writer herself, Rob is also a keen photographer, providing many pictures for Joy's books and articles.

SOCCER STARS
Rob Childs

*'We've got something very special coming here
tomorrow . . . the F.A. Cup!'*

The Swillsby Swifts are off on an Easter tour!
Their skipper, Luke Crawford, is hoping for
some terrific results – especially as he's
persuaded his talented cousin, Jon, to play for
the Swifts as a guest star.

But Jon's not going to be the only soccer star in
action: the Swifts are invited to play in a
charity tournament at which many top stars
from the past are playing an exhibition game.
And, even better, the F.A. Cup will be on
display.

There's just one problem: someone has other
plans for the cup. . .

0 440 863619

CORGI YEARLING BOOKS